D1137441

Don't miss any other
Young Corgi pony titles.

Available now:

THE PARADISE PONY
by K. M. Peyton
THE PHANTOM PONY
by Peter Clover

Also available by K. M. Peyton,
and published by Corgi Books:

For younger readers
WINDY WEBLEY

For older readers
THE SWALLOW TIALE
THE SWALLOW SUMMER
SWALLOW, THE STAR

Young Corgi Books are designed especially
with young readers in mind and are perfect
for developing reading confidence
and stamina.

The Scruffy Pony

K.M. Peyton

Illustrated by
Robin Lawrie

YOUNG CORGI BOOKS

THE SCRUFFY PONY
A YOUNG CORGI BOOK : 0 552 546224

First publication in Great Britain

PRINTING HISTORY
Young Corgi edition published 1999

3 5 7 9 10 8 6 4

Set in 16/20pt Bembo Schoolbook
by Phoenix Typesetting, Ilkley, West Yorkshire.

Young Corgi Books are published by Transworld Publishers,
61–63 Uxbridge Road, London W5 5SA,
a division of The Random House Group Ltd,
in Australia by Random House Australia (Pty) Ltd,
20 Alfred Street, Milsons Point, Sydney, NSW 2061, Australia,
in New Zealand by Random House New Zealand Ltd,
18 Poland Road, Glenfield, Auckland 10, New Zealand
and in South Africa by Random House (Pty) Ltd,
Endulini, 5a Jubilee Road, Parktown 2193, South Africa.

Printed and bound in Great Britain by
Cox & Wyman Ltd, Reading, Berkshire

Chapter One

Carrie rode back to the stable on her pony, Red Robin – down under the trees along the curving, peaty path. She was so happy she felt she would burst. So lucky! Red Robin was magic.

"He's a treasure!" they all said at the livery stable.

Red Robin was as good as he was beautiful. He was chestnut with a white star. He was very elegant, and he had good manners. He didn't bolt or buck or kick or go backwards. Carrie was the only little girl at the stable who was allowed to ride out on her own. She loved going through the woods and across the fields that belonged to the livery stable. She had learnt to ride well and everyone knew that Red Robin could be trusted.

At first they had said, behind her back, "Fancy paying that much for a pony!" That was Danielle, who was always jealous and catty. Danielle had a dark bay pony called, very suitably, Mischief. Mischief was also very beautiful, but he was as naughty as he was beautiful. He quite often bucked her off. And if he galloped he would sometimes do a sudden swerve and his rider would go straight on and land with a crump on the grass. All this made Danielle rather bad-tempered. She wasn't as good a rider as Carrie. She was too forceful and unsympathetic. And her pony wasn't to be trusted like Red Robin.

Sylvie, the girl who ran the livery stable, said, "Red Robin was very expensive but he is worth every penny." She had found Red Robin and told Carrie's father to buy him. "You don't find many like him."

Carrie knew she was very lucky. She was an only child and her parents bought her everything she wanted. Her father was a successful businessman and loved to spoil his daughter. He had to have the best. But Carrie had a giving nature and did not behave like a spoilt child. Sometimes, in fact – although she never said this – she wished she could keep Red Robin at home and look after him herself. The livery stable was expensive, but when she went to ride Red Robin was always groomed and ready for her. She never had to muck him out or clean his tack or put his bed down. Her father thought this was grand. "Who wants to do all the dirty work? You just enjoy him, my girl – thank your lucky stars we can pay for it!"

But sometimes Carrie wished she had Red Robin at home, where she could look out of her bedroom window and

see him grazing. She liked grooming
him, but he was always so sparkling
there was no need. She even liked
mucking out, making the stable tidy, but
when she started to do it Sylvie always
sent someone to take over.

Carrie didn't want to seem
ungrateful, so she didn't say anything.
Perhaps that was why she liked riding
on her own so much – because nobody
came between her and her pony. He was
completely hers, and she was in charge.
She loved the feeling of just the two of
them, cantering over the soft turf
without a care in the world. Nobody
else seemed to enjoy their pony as much
as she did.

"You are lucky!" they all said.

Carrie joined in the lessons twice a

week. Not many of the ponies jumped as well as Red Robin. They refused or ran out or clattered the poles down, but Red Robin always went over neatly, like a little cat.

"Anyone could ride Red Robin. He's so easy," Danielle said crossly, after Mischief had run out three times.

Carrie supposed it was true, but Sylvie said rather sharply, "He's not a robot, Danielle! He is very happy with his rider and wants to please. Ask yourself how Mischief feels about your riding."

It was true that Danielle was a rough rider. And when Mischief *did* behave and jump well Danielle never patted him or told him he was a good boy.

Carrie tried to feel sorry for Danielle but Sylvie said it was Danielle's own fault – she didn't want to learn. Sylvie was very patient. Not all her customers were as willing and cheerful as Carrie.

When Carrie came back from her ride she took Red Robin into his stable and took off his saddle and bridle. She rubbed the sweat marks off his back and led him out to his paddock. It was summer and the ponies grazed out at night, and came into the cool of the stable in the daytime. Carrie loved to watch Red Robin walk away down the field, sniffing at the grass, swishing his tail. She wished she could build her own house at the end, and watch him from her window when she was in bed. This was almost the best part of the ride, turning him out in the field and watching him, knowing she owned the best pony in the world.

Chapter Two

When she had finished riding, her
mother came and fetched her in the car.
She looked worried and didn't say
much. This was unusual, but Carrie was
still thinking of Red Robin and didn't
notice.

She said, "Sylvie says I can ride him
in the Hylands show next month."

And instead of saying "How lovely!"
as usual, her mother said, "We'll have
to see."

"Why will we?"

But her mother didn't answer.

Carrie was surprised. But later in the evening when her father came home she noticed there was a very gloomy feel in the house. Her parents were quiet and sad. Carrie felt something was wrong but did not like to ask. Usually her father asked her how Red Robin was, and whether she had had a good ride. But today he said nothing at all.

The next day when Carrie went to school her father was still in bed. This was very strange.

Carrie asked, "Is Daddy ill?"

"No," said her mother. "He's just having a rest."

Her father never had a rest.

But in the evening Carrie forgot all about it when she went to ride Red Robin. It was a quiet golden evening. She cantered through the green woods feeling that happy feeling again, like

bursting. She sang, and talked to Red
Robin. When she put him out in his field
he nuzzled her hand before he walked
away, as if to say, "Thank you."

But the next day her father stayed in bed again. Her mother said he was tired, but Carrie was worried.

When she came home from school in the afternoon her mother was very quiet again and said, "Carrie, I have to tell you something."

"What is it?" Carrie was frightened.

"You know you have been a very lucky little girl, all your life. Your father and I have been lucky too. But now our luck has turned. Your father has lost his money and things will have to change."

"Change how?"

"We will have to sell this house and go and live somewhere cheaper."

"I don't mind!"

Her mother looked very sad. "I'm afraid we won't be able to keep Red Robin at Sylvie's any more. It's too expensive."

"I can keep him myself! I will do all the work! It won't cost a penny!"

Carrie's heart leapt at the thought — just what she had always wanted!

But her mother looked sadder still. She said, very softly, "No, Carrie. You don't understand. Red Robin will have to be sold. You won't be able to keep him at all."

Carrie couldn't believe it. She didn't care at all about having a smaller, cheaper house — but no Red Robin! She couldn't imagine it. "We can't sell him!"

"We need the money, Carrie. I told you, our luck has run out. Life is like that sometimes."

Carrie tried not to make a fuss. She just felt as if she were shrinking, as if she had had weed-killer poured over her. She felt like a little cold stone. She could not say anything. Her tongue was dead.

Later on, she supposed it was just as bad for her mother losing her beautiful house. But a house had no heart, Carrie thought. It was just a thing. Her parents went to look at others. Their smart house was for sale and people came to look at it. Carrie had to keep her bedroom very tidy and not drop her school clothes on the floor. Sylvie was told to sell Red Robin.

"That will be easy enough," she said. "Danielle's parents will buy him. They will pay whatever you ask."

Not only had her good luck run out, Carrie thought, but her bad luck was worse than she had ever imagined. Danielle to own Red Robin! She cried and cried when she went to bed. She could not bear to think of it. Her mother stopped taking her to Sylvie's. Red Robin was sold to Danielle.

Chapter Three

After Red Robin was sold Carrie went quiet and listless. She cried a lot, alone in her room. Her parents knew what was wrong and were very worried, but they could do nothing to help. They sold their smart house and told Carrie they had found another one.

"It needs a lot doing to it. It's in the country, I'm afraid. You'll be a long way from your school friends."

At least — the only good thing — she

didn't have to change her school.

The house was a very shabby farm cottage down a quiet lane. It wasn't pretty and the garden was overgrown. At the bottom of the garden were some old sheds and a smell of chicken manure. Hardly any of their furniture would fit in and it went away to be sold. Their two big cars were sold and an old banger replaced them.

Carrie really didn't mind about losing all these things. She only missed Red Robin. She quite liked her new bedroom looking out over a field of cabbages. She had to walk up the lane every morning and catch the school bus instead of going by car. That was more fun. The farm had a dog called Big Red and a black cat with kittens.

But nothing made up for losing Red Robin. Carrie pinned her photos of him all round her bedroom wall, and hung up her rosettes.

Her father was still at home, and worked hard decorating the old cottage and clearing out the garden. Strangely, he seemed quite happy – much happier than Carrie.

He said, "Life has its up and downs, Carrie. We started without any money, before you were born. Now we're back to square one. We have to start again. Cheer up, chicken, it's not the end of the world."

But, in a way, it was. Red Robin had been her world.

When her father had cut the waist-high grass in the back garden Carrie went to explore the old sheds. Whoever had lived here last had kept chickens, and stored junk. One shed was full of empty oil drums, old lawn-mowers, flower pots and boxes. It had a window high up filled with elder flowers from a tree outside. It smelled musty, of old hay.

When Carrie examined it properly she realized that this shed had once been a stable. Running along the wall at the back was an old wooden manger, its edge worn smooth by the necks of horses eating. There was a ring in the wall to tie up to, and on the floor there were old stable flagstones, with a drain in the middle. She pictured it empty, cleared of its rubbish.

She started to drag all the rubbish out through the door. She was so excited her father came to see what all the activity was about.

"Look!" Carrie cried. "A real stable!"

Just as she had always dreamed! She could look out of her bedroom window right into the stable. There was no Red Robin – but at least there was a stable!

"Well, perhaps you could make
yourself a little house here," her father
said, surprised by her excitement.

"Not a house, a stable," Carrie said.

"But we can't buy you a pony,
love," her father reminded her.

Her parents tried to persuade her to
make a little house. She was so keen
on the old shed. They offered her an
old table and chair, and a nice rug.

But Carrie refused the offer. "It's a *stable*," she insisted.

When the rubbish was cleared away, she swept the floor. She used the broom to knock down all the cobwebs, right up to the ceiling. She cleaned out the manger, and threw buckets of water over the dusty flags. Her father gave her a big tin of emulsion paint and a large brush, and she painted all the inside white. (Also most of herself.) Her father did the high bits for her, standing on a ladder. They painted the doors with a dark green gloss, and oiled the hinges. When it was finished it was a sparkling stable, good enough for the best of Sylvie's ponies.

"There," Carrie said, beaming. All the work had made her cheeks pink again.

But her father was worried. He thought she had done it to get Red Robin back. "It's no good," he said. "It's an *empty* stable."

Carrie said, "I know."

Her father didn't understand. The empty stable was better than nothing. To have a beautiful stable at the bottom of her garden was something she had always wanted. It was a step back to her old happiness. A little step.

Chapter Four

Now she had the stable, she just had to imagine Red Robin back there, as she had always dreamed. Somehow it was comforting. She fetched two bales of straw from the farm, and put a thick bed down, and the farmer gave her a bale of hay.

"Going to have a pony, are you?" he said.

"No. Just the stable," Carrie replied.

The farmer was puzzled but didn't say anything.

"She's a funny little thing, that Carrie," he said to his wife. "Made that old loose box fit for a Derby winner. But they haven't got a horse!"

"I think she used to have a pony. Her mother said she did. Broke her heart when they had to sell it. They can't afford one now."

The farmer didn't say anything, but he stored the news at the back of his mind. Animals were good for children, he thought. He had always had a dog when he was a boy. And rabbits and mice, and a donkey for a bit. Now he had a herd of cows and a milk quota and not much time for anything else.

He didn't think any more about it until, two weeks later, he went to market with some sheep to sell. It was the week before Christmas, and it was raining hard. In the market were a few horses for sale and, at the end of the row, a small, thin pony tucked up against the rain. It looked tired and sick and the farmer could not imagine that anyone would bid for it.

He heard someone say, "Looks like it wants a bit of tender loving care."

And suddenly the farmer thought of Carrie and her empty stable. Just what this little fellow could do with!

He went up to the pony and untied it and walked it up and down. It wasn't lame. It didn't bite him or attempt to kick. When he tied it back on the rail, it gave him a sad nuzzle with its soft nose and heaved a sigh.

Perhaps I'm a sentimental ass, the farmer thought. Why would the lass want a scruffy thing like this?

But he had a kind heart and decided it was worth a try. If she didn't want it he could put it in the cow byre and give it some grub. When it was fat and healthy he could bring it back to sell again. No skin off his nose.

So when the pony came into the ring and nobody made a bid, the farmer offered a small price and the pony was his. He loaded it into his sheep-van and drove it home. He stopped outside Carrie's cottage and went and knocked at the door.

Carrie wasn't home from school yet.

Her parents were there, decorating the hallway. He told them what he'd done. They both looked very doubtful.

"We can't afford to keep a pony," Carrie's father said. "That's the trouble."

"Why, I can let you have some hay and grass. That's all this little fellow needs. And you've got that grand stable. It might cheer her up, like, to have a pony to look after. Her Christmas present from me. It needn't cost you, not with me next door."

Carrie's parents had always found keeping Red Robin very expensive. They found it hard to believe that it could be as cheap as the farmer said.

"I suppose Sylvie's place was very smart. But how will Carrie cope with doing it by herself?"

The farmer could not understand this. "Of course she will! It's what it's all about, cosseting and cuddling – puppies, kittens, ponies – looking after 'em. Kids love it. Keeps 'em out of mischief. Shall I put 'im in the stable for you, then?"

"Well, yes, all right." It seemed rude to refuse.

But when they saw the pony, Carrie's mum and dad were dismayed. They tried not to show it. "It's very kind of you," they said.

When the farmer had gone her father said, "It looks like a carpet."

"A dirty old carpet. I expect it's got fleas."

"Whatever was he thinking of, buying it for Carrie?"

"It's nothing but a skinny rabbit."

"It's rubbish."

They went out with an umbrella and stood looking doubtfully over the stable door. The pony was munching the hay the farmer had piled in the hayrack. He didn't take any notice of them. He was a dirty brown colour, with a mane and tail full of mud. The rain ran off his coat in rivulets and every now and then he shivered.

"Poor little thing," said Carrie's mum. "He's cold. He needs a blanket."

"Red Robin had rugs, didn't he?" Carrie's dad remembered.

"Sylvie kept them. I might find that old car rug of Grandpa's. That would do."

She went indoors and came back with a tartan rug. They put it over the pony's back and fastened it on with two belts buckled together. The pony went on munching.

They waited for Carrie to come home from school, full of excitement at the present they had in store for her.

Chapter Five

When Carrie came in they said, "We've got a surprise for you. Go and look in your stable."

Carrie's face was shocked. "What is it?"

"Go and see."

Carrie's eyes lit with excitement. It could only mean one thing! She had built her stable for Red Robin and Red Robin would be there! Her heart flooded with a fantastic joy. She thought she would burst! She dashed out of the room and down the garden.

Too late, her mother realized what had happened. Carrie thought Red Robin had come back. "Oh dear, what have we done?"

She ran down the garden after Carrie and saw her lean over the half door. "Carrie! Carrie!" She wanted to warn her.

But it was too late.

To Carrie the disappointment was like an axe-blow. Her vision of darling Red Robin all shining and welcoming was shattered. All she saw was a dirty, muddy rump and a matted tail, a vision utterly unlike the one she was expecting.

Her joy turned to bitter disappointment. "What's that horrid thing doing in my lovely stable?" she shouted.

Her mother was shocked. "Carrie, it's a present. Mr Hemmings, the farmer up the lane, bought him for you in the market, to look after. He's going to give you the hay and the feed. The poor little thing needs a home. He was shivering so we put that old blanket on him."

"I don't want it in my stable! My lovely stable! The pony's all dirty and scruffy."

"A stable's no good if it's empty." Carrie's mother said, bewildered.

Although Carrie was only saying what her parents had thought themselves, her mother was upset and troubled by Carrie's reaction. But Carrie had never seen a dirty pony at the livery stable – only shining expensive ponies.

"It's for you to look after," she told her.

"I don't want to," said Carrie.

The disappointment was so great she could not bear it. She rushed back into the house and up to her room and slammed the door.

Her mother and father did not know what to do. It had not turned out how they expected at all.

But Carrie's father was cross and said, "She's behaving like a spoilt brat! Only had the best all her life. She's got to learn. If she doesn't look after him, no-one else will. I'll make sure she knows that. And when he dies of starvation she'll have to go to Mr Hemmings and tell him."

He told Carrie.

She said, "I don't care! I don't care if it dies! I don't want it."

When Carrie had gone to bed, her mother said "Oh dear — what have we done?" She was very worried.

"We'll wake her in time in the morning, so that she can feed him before she goes to school. He'll be hungry then. If she knows no-one else will look after him, she'll do it."

But in the morning Carrie still refused.

Her father thought of carrying her, kicking and screaming, down the garden and making her feed the pony, but he knew it wouldn't work. He had a better plan.

He sighed, and said, "Poor little devil. All day without seeing anyone. No food and no water!" Another sigh. "Off you go then, Carrie. Have a good day."

He took her down the lane to meet the school bus. Carrie didn't say

anything. The bus came and she got on
without a word.

Her father walked home, really
worried.

"I'm afraid we handled it all wrong,"
her mother said. "She thought it was
going to be Red Robin. Oh dear, what
do we do now?"

"I'm not sure."

"We can feed him perhaps, and not
tell her. She won't know."

"No." Carrie's father was a stubborn
man. "No. We mustn't give in to her.
She's got to learn. This pony is her
responsibility. He'll get nothing if she
doesn't feed him."

Meanwhile Carrie, at school, was
thinking what a mean and nasty trick
her parents had played on her.

Pretending Red Robin had come back! Every time she thought of looking over the stable door and seeing, instead of dear Robin, that scruffy pony, tears came into her eyes.

"Is anything wrong, dear," her teacher asked anxiously.

"No." Carrie swallowed back her tears. "It's – it's just hayfever."

And when she got home she didn't go down the garden even to look at the pony but went up to her room and slammed the door.

Chapter Six

Her mother had had a terrible day, not
feeding the poor pony. She had gone
down to look at him and he had put his
head over the door and made a little
knuckering noise in his nostrils. His hay
was all gone, his water bucket was
empty and the bedding was dirty. The
blanket had fallen off and was trodden
into the straw. Carrie's mother nearly
cried. She gave him a little water in the
bottom of the bucket and the pony

drank it all thirstily, but she daren't give
him any more. Her husband really
meant what he said!

When she had made tea and they
were all sitting round the table she said,
"I'm really worried about that pony."
She wasn't just saying it for Carrie. She
meant it. Her voice shook. "He looked
so sad, peering over the door. He
whinnied to me."

"He must be pretty hungry by now,"
her husband said. "But that's his bad
luck, isn't it?"

"I could feed him tonight, if Carrie
doesn't want to."

"You will not."

Both Carrie and her mother knew
that tone of voice. No-one dared say
any more when he spoke like that.
Carrie darted a glance at her mother.
Her mother looked as miserable as the
scruffy pony.

Carrie told herself that it was just a

bad trick being played on her by her parents to make her do as she was told. She went up to her room to play with her model ponies. But she could not help glancing out of the window to see if the pony was looking over the door. But there was no sign of him. Perhaps he had died . . . She thought of him lying on the floor, dead. Her eyes stung with tears. Then she remembered – it was just a trick! The pony wasn't Red Robin.

When she went to bed she cried after her mother had kissed her goodnight. Her mother was just as miserable as she was.

The hungry pony, who thought his luck had changed, was now resigned to the fact that it hadn't. He had a raging thirst, and his tummy rumbled emptily. He ate some of his straw bedding but it was too dirty. He tried to open the bolt on the door with his teeth, so that he could get at the lovely grass in the gar-

den, but it was too stiff. Looking at the lovely grass made him even more miserable, so he turned his head into the corner of the stable and shut his eyes. He had forgotten how, long ago, he had cavorted with his mother in a lovely green field. He only remembered being sold into hunger and ill-treatment. Even yesterday's lovely hay was now only a memory. He sighed and shivered. His thirst was terrible.

Chapter Seven

Carrie didn't sleep very well. She
dreamed that Red Robin was starving,
shut in a dirty stable with nothing to eat
and drink. She woke up with a start. It
was just getting light. She knew, after the
panic in her dream, that Red Robin was
still at Sylvie's and now belonged to
Danielle. And she slumped back on her
pillow with the familiar sad ache that
always came to her when she thought of
Red Robin. But on top of it there was

another worry – a deep, real worry
which for some moments she could not
account for. The she remembered! There
was a starving pony. But it wasn't Red
Robin. It was the new pony, the one
spoiling her lovely stable.

She turned over and groaned. "I
won't!" she determined. "They can't
make me love that thing!"

But she could not sleep. She felt truly
awful. Perhaps she was ill. That would
account for it. But it was only her brain
that was ill. Her body was great, her
cheeks pink and her eyes bright.

She dressed and went slowly down to
breakfast.

Her mother looked terrible.

"You've just time to feed your pony
before the school bus," her father said. "If
you hurry."

"It's not my pony," Carrie muttered.

"Poor little beast." Her father shook
his head. "No-one else is going to do it."

"I— " started her mother.

"You will NOT," said her father in that voice. "Carrie will do it or no-one will."

Carrie tried to eat her toast but it stuck in her throat.

"Come on," said her father. "Get your coat or you'll miss the bus."

Carrie looked at the clock. There wasn't time to go down to the stable now, even if she wanted to. She choked down her last mouthful and ran out of the kitchen. She put her coat on blindly and went out of the house.

On the bus she wouldn't talk to anyone, but turned her head to look out of the window. The fields were full of rich grass and happy cows and horses grazing contentedly. The tears stung her eyes.

"Your hayfever is worse," said her teacher. "You should go the doctor and get some treatment for it."

Carrie could not concentrate. The day went past as if it were a week long. She kept thinking of that scruffy pony lying dead in her lovely stable. Even a dirty old pony like that didn't deserve such a fate. She would be reported to the RSPCA and have to go to court! That nice farmer would be shocked and wouldn't speak to her any more. Luckily she hadn't seen him since he had delivered the pony. But she couldn't expect to miss him every day.

When she got off the bus that afternoon she ran down the lane.

However, as she reached the door she checked herself, remembering it was a trick. But she felt so miserable. Her father was out, looking for a job, and her mother said she was just going down the lane to post a letter. She didn't say anything about the pony.

"I'll be ten minutes," she said as she went out.

Carrie looked out of the kitchen door. There was no head peering over the stable door. He must be dead! Carrie started to cry again. She could not bear the way she was starting to feel about herself.

But both her parents were out, and now was the perfect chance to go and see. She only had a few minutes before her mother came back. She went out of the back door and crept down the garden path, her heart hammering with fear. "Please don't be dead, pony," she prayed. She couldn't bear it.

Chapter Eight

But just before she got to the stable an enquiring nose poked over the door. Carrie saw the pony's nostrils give a ripple of welcome exactly like Robin's had done. And large anxious eyes gazed at her from beneath the matted forelock, every bit as speaking as Robin's had been. "Please feed me," they said, without a doubt. *Please!*

The stable was filthy, the empty bucket upturned. Carrie ran into the

shed where the bale of hay was kept and tugged off a large slice and threw it over the door. Then she grabbed the bucket, filled it at the tap and dragged it into the stable. The pony turned from the hay and plunged his lips into the water.

Carrie ran.

When her mother came back from the post-box, Carrie was upstairs playing with her model ponies. Her face was flushed, but she wouldn't speak. Her mother brought her some biscuits and a glass of orange juice. Carrie's heart was crashing so hard she thought her mother would hear it. She didn't know if she was very happy or furious — it was such a mix! She kept seeing the pony's face over the door and the little anxious fluttering of his nostrils. But she wouldn't say anything to her mother. She was worried now that she hadn't given the pony enough hay — that little bit wouldn't last long.

When her father came home he didn't say anything about the pony. He talked to her mother about job-hunting and seemed upset. Carrie kept quiet. Her head was in a whirl. She could not work out how she felt now about the new pony, but she kept seeing his face over the door and the look in his eyes. She knew then that – even if she didn't want him – she could not neglect him.

But she wouldn't say so.

Her parents didn't say any more about the pony and when Carrie's mother came to tuck her up she didn't say anything either. But Carrie could not stop thinking about him. Once more she couldn't get to sleep. She heard her mother and father come to bed. It was a fine night and a full moon was shining. Carrie got out of bed and went to the window. All was silent and there was no sign of life in her stable. The moon shone across the fields and woods and nothing

stirred, and the sky was full of stars.
Carrie felt funny looking at it.

She wished she could see the pony
looking out. But he wasn't. Perhaps he
was asleep. Or, if she hadn't given him
enough hay, perhaps he was dying
again.

She knew she wouldn't go back to
sleep again if she went back to bed, so
very quietly she put on some clothes and
her boots and went downstairs. She let
herself out and walked out into the
garden. It was cold and the air was

damp, and she was rather frightened. It looked so different in the moonlight. And so still! Like a quite different place.

But her stable stood four-square at the bottom of the garden, its fresh paint gleaming in the light of the moon.

Carrie went to the door and peered in. The pony was lying down. When Carrie's form loomed in the doorway he

scrambled hastily to his feet and cowered in the far corner of the box. She had frightened him. And she could see that he expected a blow or a harsh word.

How thin he was! In the sharp white light each rib made a shadow, so that he looked almost like a striped zebra. All the hay had gone and the water bucket was empty. The lovely stable stank of manure.

Carrie stood looking for a long time. Her feelings were in such a mix! The pony stopped looking frightened and turned his head curiously. Carrie noticed that his head was pretty under the matted forelock. He had a little white star between his eyes, just like Red Robin.

Carrie slid back the bolt and went into the stable. It was really stinky – Sylvie would never let a stable get like this! Carrie felt ashamed. She went up to the pony and put her hand on his dirty neck.

"Poor skinny rabbit. Perhaps I will look after you. Just until I get Red Robin back."

He could be a stop-gap pony, until her father got rich again. He was bound to get another job soon. He always got what he wanted.

"I'll call you Skinny Rabbit. Because you are."

The pony nuzzled at her hand. Carrie laid her cheek against the scrawny neck and put her arms around him. He smelled just the same as Red Robin, in spite of the dirt.

"I'm sorry," she whispered.

Chapter Nine

When she said she was sorry, Carrie felt
a little jump of pleasure inside at the
words. The pony had fallen on hard
days, like her dad. She could make him
better.

She gave the pony some more hay
and refilled the water bucket, and went
back to bed, leaving Skinny Rabbit
munching eagerly.

She set her alarm clock carefully. She
wanted to have time to muck out the

stable before she went to school. She had never done it before but she had seen the grooms doing it at Sylvie's. Her father had a wheelbarrow and a garden fork, so it shouldn't be beyond her.

It was – nearly. When she opened the door to get the wheelbarrow in, Skinny Rabbit tried to come out. He had his eye on the grass outside. She pushed him back just in time and went to look for a halter, but there wasn't one. In the end she put a bit of old washing-line round his neck and tied it to the manger. It wasn't correct, but it worked. Even then he was still standing on a lot of the dirty straw.

Carrie forked what she could into the wheelbarrow, and then had to back it out and try to make the pony move over. She said, "Move over!" like Sylvie's grooms, but nothing happened. The pony just looked at her pathetically.

Time was moving on. She did her

best, but the stable looked nothing like Red Robin's, with the clean straw forked round the edges and all the dirty straw removed. Certainly it was cleaner, but that was all. Carrie threw some clean straw on top and that helped. She threw down some more hay, topped up the bucket and ran.

Her parents made no remarks at all. But when Carrie had gone to school they flung their arms round each other with relief.

During the day they let the pony out on what they called their 'lawn', a good square of thick grass. The pony put down his head and tore at the lovely feed.

"Well, who knows?" said Carrie's dad. "It might work the miracle."

At school, Carrie no longer had hayfever, but seemed to be living in a dream.

"Wake up, Carrie dear," said her teacher anxiously.

Carrie jumped. Somehow she could not stop thinking about that funny pony. If she really looked after him, could he ever get as fat and shiny as Red Robin? In her mind the skinny rabbit grew and blossomed and cantered with her down shady rides through the woods, and won rosettes at all the shows. Her dream would not go away.

But when she got home she was shocked to see what a poor little thing he was. Her dreams had run on out of control. He would never be another Red Robin! But having the stable to clean was something she enjoyed. And her mother gave her an old clothes brush and she tried her hand at grooming. It didn't seem to make any difference. The pony looked the same but Carrie was so dirty she had to go and have a bath.

Chapter Ten

On Saturday morning Mr Hemmings called in.

"How's the little fellow then? Glad to have a nice home, I'll bet."

They were so pleased to see him, as they now realized they knew very little about looking after ponies. Where did you buy a proper brush? How could they stop him knocking the water bucket over? How much hay should he have? How did you tie a pony up?

Where could they get a halter?
Shouldn't he have more exercise?
Could Carrie ride him?

Mr Hemmings scratched his head. "Well, he needs to get stronger first. First thing is to get him fit. You have a very nice stable here but the little fellow will be happier if he's out in a field. There's nothing beats grass and freedom for a pony that's been locked up with no food. You can put him in with my cows in the daytime, if you like."

The cows were just across the lane, no distance at all. The gate was opposite their cottage.

Mr Hemmings gave them a halter, and showed them how to catch the pony in the evening. "He'll come to you when he knows there's a titbit waiting. Catch him with a carrot, or a bucket with a bit of feed in it. Then when you're back in the stable he'll find a bucket of feed waiting and you'll have no trouble. He'll come to you as soon as he sees you."

He gave them a bag of feed. It sounded easy.

"You have any trouble, then you just send for me."

So Skinny Rabbit went out in the field across the road. Carrie found it was easy to put him out in the morning, then muck out the empty stable. She learned how to do it properly, to leave it all ready for evening with a bed of clean straw. When she came home from school and went to the gate with her halter, Skinny Rabbit would come trotting over to be collected. She really looked forward to catching him again in the evening, and hearing his funny little whinny of welcome.

And after a week or two his ribs
stopped showing and his coat lost its
dead look and took on a natural shine.

"We can hardly call him Skinny Rabbit any more," Carrie's mother said. "Because he isn't."

"Just Rabbit," Carrie said.

Everything was different now. Carrie had stopped thinking about Red Robin all the time and was now thinking about when she could ride Rabbit.

But Mr Hemmings was a bit doubtful. "Now, we don't know as how he rides," he said. "Maybe for riding he's not too good."

Like Mischief, Carrie thought, who always bucked Danielle off. But Rabbit didn't look naughty. Mr Hemmings was being careful, she knew, because it would be his fault if Rabbit bucked her off and she got hurt.

"I don't mind if I get hurt," she assured him.

"It shouldn't come to that! But you have to go slow in these things. It pays to go slow and careful. Then no-one gets hurt."

"She's a good little rider," Carrie's mother said.

Mr Hemmings found a saddle that was too big and a bridle that was too small in his back barn, and said they would 'make do' for the time being. He let out all the holes on the bridle and put a thick blanket under the saddle. Rabbit didn't seem to mind.

"I'll hold him now and you get on his back. Get up from the garden wall so the saddle doesn't move, and sit down quietly."

Carrie did as she was told. Rabbit stood still and did not even toss his head.

"Aye, he knows his job," Mr Hemmings said happily.

Carrie rode Rabbit up and down the garden. He started with a touch from her heels and stopped when asked, and circled to the left and to the right.

"That's a right well-mannered little pony," Mr Hemmings said, even more happily. He had been afraid that he might have bought what he called a "bad 'un". "You aren't to know till you get aboard."

Then he decided, "You ride him down the lane now to my yard, and you can take him round my orchard till you get the feel of him."

Carrie was thrilled to be back on a pony again. Rabbit was nothing like Red Robin. He didn't bounce like Red Robin, and his neck seemed very low down and long in front of her. But his paces were very smooth and comfortable. She had to admit that his trot was *more* comfortable, not so jiggy.

When she took him back to his stable, she decided to wash his mane and tail. It was a warm day and Mr Hemmings said it would do no harm to give him a bath all over. So her mother helped her and Rabbit stood quite happily, covered in soap-suds, and Carrie's father hosed him down afterwards with the garden hose. He didn't mind at all. Carrie remembered that when Sylvie bathed Red Robin, Red Robin had been extremely naughty, kicking in all directions. She didn't remember it out loud – only to herself.

When he was dry Rabbit was all shiny. He was a dark brown in colour (now that you could see), with brighter brown bits round his eyes and muzzle, and faint dapples on his quarters. His mane and tail were thick and black. Carrie brushed him hard and his coat lay clean and gleaming. His ribs didn't stand out any more.

"Well, he wouldn't win prizes, but you wouldn't know him from the skinny rabbit he used to be," her father said.

Chapter Eleven

As summer came Carrie would take
Rabbit out in the evenings after school.
She soon grew out of riding in the
orchard and started to explore round Mr
Hemmings's fields, following the tractor
tracks and finding paths through the
woods.

One day Carrie's mother met Sylvie
when she was shopping. Sylvie asked
after Carrie and Carrie's mother told
her about the pony.

"It's only a poor thing, really, but she seems quite happy now she can ride again. She's stopped moping over Red Robin."

"I think Red Robin's coming up for sale again soon," Sylvie said. "Danielle's getting too big for him. She's never been happy with him really – they've never got on too well together, I'm afraid. There would be a chance to buy him back."

"If we had the money . . ." Carrie's mother said.

"He won't be cheap, I'm afraid."

But a week later Carrie's father got a new job. It was a very good one. He came home and they all went for dinner to celebrate – Carrie too.

"We'll be back just like we used to be!" he said, smiling. "A nice house again – we'll go looking tomorrow – and you can have riding lessons again, Carrie."

"Back at Sylvie's, Carrie, just like you've always wanted! And even Red Robin—" But Carrie's mother stopped herself, just in case. He might already be sold to someone else.

"Red Robin? What about Rabbit?"

"Oh, Mr Hemmings could have Rabbit back," her father said. "He owns him, after all. Let's face it, Carrie, you won't win any prizes on Rabbit."

Carrie went rather quiet after that.

When they got home she went down to her stable to say goodnight to Rabbit, as she always did. He was eating his hay out of the hayrack, but turned round and came to the door when he saw her. As he always did. His nose rippled with greeting.

Carrie stroked his muzzle. She loved to feel the softness of it. "You're mine really. Not Mr Hemmings's. I don't care what Daddy says."

She wanted to tell Rabbit she would keep him always, but she could not help remembering the fuss she had made about losing Red Robin. She had cried for weeks. Now she maybe had the chance to buy him back. It ought to make her feel very happy. But somehow it didn't. She was very confused.

Mr Hemmings had always said that if Rabbit was no use he could always go back to the market and be sold. That is what would happen to him. And who would buy him? How did she know it wouldn't be another person who would starve him and hit him? Because he wasn't a prize-winner – only a rather ordinary pony. A two-a-penny pony. Not like Red Robin. Could she take Rabbit to Sylvie's? Or would they all laugh at her common pony?

Her father would think she was mad. He always liked the best, and now he would be able to afford it again.

And besides, Carrie thought, she liked looking after her own pony now. She even liked mucking out. It was really satisfying to see the stable all clean and fresh with new straw, and to see Rabbit

pulling happily at his hay; to know that she had done it all and made him comfortable. She doubted if her father would understand that.

"Why do it yourself when you can pay someone to do it for you?" he used to say when he was rich.

Carrie had come to like the cottage and the fields and Mr Hemmings's farmyard and the view from her bed of the stable at the bottom of the garden. Her own stable! She had never missed having her own bathroom, which her parents seemed to think was terribly important.

A small, steely part of her was set against her father's plans. She realized she didn't want to change anything. As she buried her face in Rabbit's thick mane she realized she didn't really want Red Robin back. She loved Rabbit! How terrible – her father would never understand her change of heart!

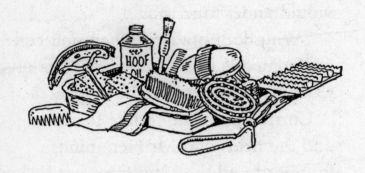

Chapter Twelve

Her parents were now looking for a nice house back where they had lived before, and quite soon Danielle's father approached them about buying Red Robin back. Luckily Carrie's father never agreed a price until he had argued a lot about it, so he laughed when Danielle's father told him how much he wanted and said, "You must be joking, mate."

Danielle's father just smiled and no decision was taken.

"I'm glad, because I don't want Red Robin back," Carrie said.

Her father stared at her as if she were mad. "You don't want Red Robin—! After all the fuss we had! All those tears! Have you lost your senses?"

"I want to keep Rabbit," Carrie whispered.

"But Red Robin's a winner – he's worth ten of Rabbit!"

Carrie could find nothing to say. She felt frozen up in inside. She knew her father would win. He always did.

"Oh, Carrie dear," her mother said. "You know how you loved it at Sylvie's – how happy you were! Don't be so silly!"

But Carrie knew that her mother liked it at Sylvie's too, taking her in the car and waiting, and talking to the other mothers, watching her having lessons, proud of her daughter's progress. They were all like that at Sylvie's. Her mother wouldn't be as proud of her on Rabbit as she would if she were on Red Robin.

But it took a while to find the right house, and no-one else would buy Red Robin because he now had rather a bad reputation, so Carrie was able to go on riding Rabbit in the country. But the more she rode him, the more she loved him, the more she wanted things to stay the same.

But how could they?

Carrie's father eventually found a large smart house standing in a lot of garden not far from where they had lived before. Carrie looked at the garden with interest. It was so big you could keep a pony in it. She said this but her parents laughed and told her not to be silly. The road was quiet and led into woods and common land. She could be happy here with Rabbit! But they told her not to be silly.

Carrie scowled. "I want my stable," she said. "In the garden."

They gaped at her.

She said, "It's *my* stable. I painted it and made it nice. I want it. It would easily move. The removal men can bring it. It's just a waste, leaving it behind."

Her parents humoured her. "I suppose it would be simple enough. Stick it down the bottom and no-one would see it."

Carrie's heart leapt. She did not dare say she wanted Rabbit in it – not yet. But she implored Mr Hemmings not to sell him. "Not yet! He won't cost you anything, will he, in with the cows? You won't send him to market, will you? *Please!*"

"There's no hurry, love, no. I don't mind keeping him a bit. I won't send him to market."

If Mr Hemmings guessed at Carrie's feelings, he didn't say anything. He thought her mum and dad didn't know a lot about animals. Or children either, come to that. But they meant well.

He said all that Carrie wanted to hear. She could get the bus back to the farm on Saturdays and ride him after she had been to Sylvie's for her lesson. The future was not entirely black.

But her father had at last agreed on a price for Red Robin, and it was arranged that he would stay at Sylvie's as before.

"We'll have him vetted, and Carrie can give him a spin to see nothing's wrong, and the deal will be done."

Carrie's father was pleased with the way everything was going. They moved house, uprooted Carrie's stable and rebuilt it at the bottom of the garden, under the trees, and bought a new car. And Carrie had her own bathroom again. Rabbit went out with the cows as usual, but missed Carrie coming to call for him in the evenings. He would stand at the gate looking across the lane at the cottage. But the cottage was empty and quiet. After a bit he would turn away

and get on with his grazing. If Carrie
cried in bed at night, nobody heard her.

The Saturday after they moved it was
arranged that they would go down to
Sylvie's and see Red Robin.

"Let Carrie get up on him again, and
if she's happy, then it's a deal."

"What if I'm not happy?" Carrie
muttered.

But her father didn't hear.

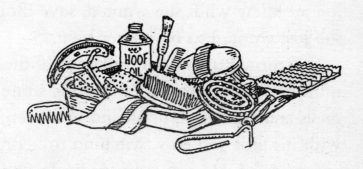

Chapter Thirteen

Seeing Red Robin again, Carrie was torn with doubts. She remembered how she had loved riding out on him and saw again what a beautiful pony he was. She got up on him and shortened her reins. Red Robin tossed his head bossily which was not likc she remembered him.

"I'll go for a ride through the woods," she said.

She didn't want to ride him in the

school with everyone watching. She wanted to sort out her brain. She no longer knew what she wanted, save that she just wanted to be on her own.

She turned away and rode out of the yard at a walk. Robin felt just the same as she remembered, bouncing and keen, with his little red ears twitching to hear every sound. He seemed very lively and she couldn't relax as she did on Rabbit. He spooked at plastic bags and

pretended he couldn't go past a fallen branch – it was too dangerous! But he did, after a minute or so. Rabbit was far more sensible, she thought.

Carrie had a canter up a long grassy ride between bracken and birch trees and all her old feelings of enjoyment in the game little pony came back to her. She hadn't cantered yet on Rabbit, because Mr Hemmings had said she should take it steady until he was strong

again. Robin had never known what it was to starve and nearly die. He had always had the best.

Carrie realized that she ought to get back to the stable as they were all waiting for her. So she turned him round and walked to the top of the long rise. Her feelings were even more mixed up now, because she was enjoying Red Robin. He was so different from Rabbit. But she enjoyed Rabbit too!

However, when she turned round Robin started to pull and fret, trying to go faster.

"Don't be stupid, Robin," she said, holding him. He had never behaved like this before. Nearly all ponies hurried up on the return journey, but not in this naughty way. He kept snatching at the reins, putting his head down crossly. She pulled him up and made him stand still. But he pranced and napped, going backwards. She was surprised and a bit worried. "Walk on then," she said, and patted his neck.

Once more he snatched at the reins. Then he gave a big buck, quite unexpectedly, so that Carrie almost came off. And before she could gather herself together he had set off at a flat gallop down the long grassy slope.

Carrie had never been bolted with before. She had no control over the pony

at all. Even when she pulled on the reins he just pulled back, stronger than her, and went faster than ever. The wide ride closed in at the bottom and the path snaked in and out of the trees; it was quite tricky even to trot here, let alone gallop. Carrie hauled frantically on Robin's mouth, but it now seemed to be made of iron, and he didn't slow down at all.

After that Carrie didn't remember much — only the fear rising in her throat as the trees closed in. She ducked down in the saddle to avoid the branches, and couldn't see the direction the path was taking. A branch whipped her face agonizingly and her eyes were full of tears. She couldn't see a thing. Then there was another crack on her helmet which threw her back in the saddle. Robin swung round a bend and she was in free fall, flying through the air. She hit a tree, and remembered nothing more.

Chapter Fourteen

When she came to she was in Sylvie's kitchen, lying on the divan where the dogs usually slept.

She had a raging headache and felt sick. She saw anxious faces all round her and couldn't remember for a bit what had happened. She heard her mother say, "I can't understand it. He used to be such a good little pony."

And Sylvie said, "I'm afraid Danielle has ruined him. It's not his fault. I knew we had problems with him these days but I never expected this. I should never have let her go out alone!"

"But she always used to."

"Ponies are only as good as their riders," Sylvie said. "A good rider makes a good pony. Robin was brilliant with Carrie before, I know. But since Danielle has been riding him—" She shook her head. "It's my fault. I didn't foresee this. I'm sure Carrie could get Robin back to how he was before, but I can see – after this – that you won't be very keen to have him."

"No way," said Carrie's father. "It's lucky we didn't pay out first!"

Carrie heard this conversation in a daze. Her father wasn't going to buy Robin! She felt big tears running out of her eyes and down her cheeks. Why was she crying? She didn't know. She could still keep dear Rabbit! She sobbed with relief. But now poor Robin might be sent to market . . .

She choked all this out to Sylvie and her mother.

They both laughed. "You are funny!"

Sylvie said "There's no problem – of course Robin won't be sent to market! There's another rider interested in him – a boy – and he knows him well and will be able to iron out his bad ways. They can't pay as much – that's why Danielle's father was keen for you to buy him. But after this I'm pretty sure he'll have him. And he'll stay here and you will be able to see him – and ride him too, I expect, when he behaves himself."

"And I can keep Rabbit?"

"For the time being that will be the best thing, I'm sure. We know Rabbit won't try and kill you!"

There was only one thing left after this. While everyone was being so nice to her Carrie decided to say it. "In my own stable?" she whispered.

There was a surprised silence.

"So I can see him out of my bedroom window? Like at the cottage?"

Her mother said doubtfully, "All that mucking out?"

"I like it."

There was another long silence.

Sylvie said gently, "I know what she means. There's nothing like looking after your own pony. That's how you really get to know and love it. She could still come down here for lessons, if she wants."

"Oh, I do want!" Carrie said. Then she could see Red Robin too!

Even her father said, "Well, we're not keen gardeners, let's face it. Half the garden could be a paddock, couldn't it?"

And the stable under the trees, with

dear Rabbit's face poking out to greet
her every morning . . . Carrie lay back,
amazed. Everything had come out right,
without her having to do anything at
all. Robin had done it for her.

Dear Red Robin! Dear Rabbit!

THE END